STONE SOUP

RETOLD BY
Heather Forest

ILLUSTRATED BY
Susan Gaber

AUGUST HOUSE
LittleFolk

This Book is dedicated to our community of friends.
– H. F. and S.G.

Book Design by Mina Greenstein.
Manufactured in Korea

10 9   PB

Library of Congress Cataloging-in-Publication Data
Forest, Heather
Stone soup / Heather Forest ; Susan Gaber [illustrator]
   p.   cm.
Summary: Two hungry travelers use a stone as a soup starter and
demonstrate the benefits of sharing. Includes a recipe for soup.
ISBN-13: 978-087483-498-7 (hc)
ISBN-13: 978-087483-602-8
[1.Folklore.] I. Gaber, Susan, ill. II. Title.
PZ8.1. F76St   1997
398.2'2 –dc21   97-10453
{E}

First Hardcover Edition, 1998
First Paperback Edition, 2000

The paper used in this publication meets the minimum requirements
of the American National Standards for Information Sciences –
permanence of Paper for Printed Library Materials, ANSI.48-1984

Author's Note

"Stone Soup" is a popular European folktale that has been told and retold for centuries. In the French version, the travelers are cast as soldiers and the townspeople are fearful of being generous because of the ravages of war. In Sweden, the story features a tramp who teaches a stingy old woman generosity by using a nail to start a sumptuous "nail broth." In the Russian version, an axe serves as the soup starter. Everywhere the tale is told, the plot ends with the optimistic realization that when each person makes a small contribution, the collective impact can be huge.

This contemporary version of "Stone Soup" takes place in a village located anywhere that people learn about the pleasures of sharing.

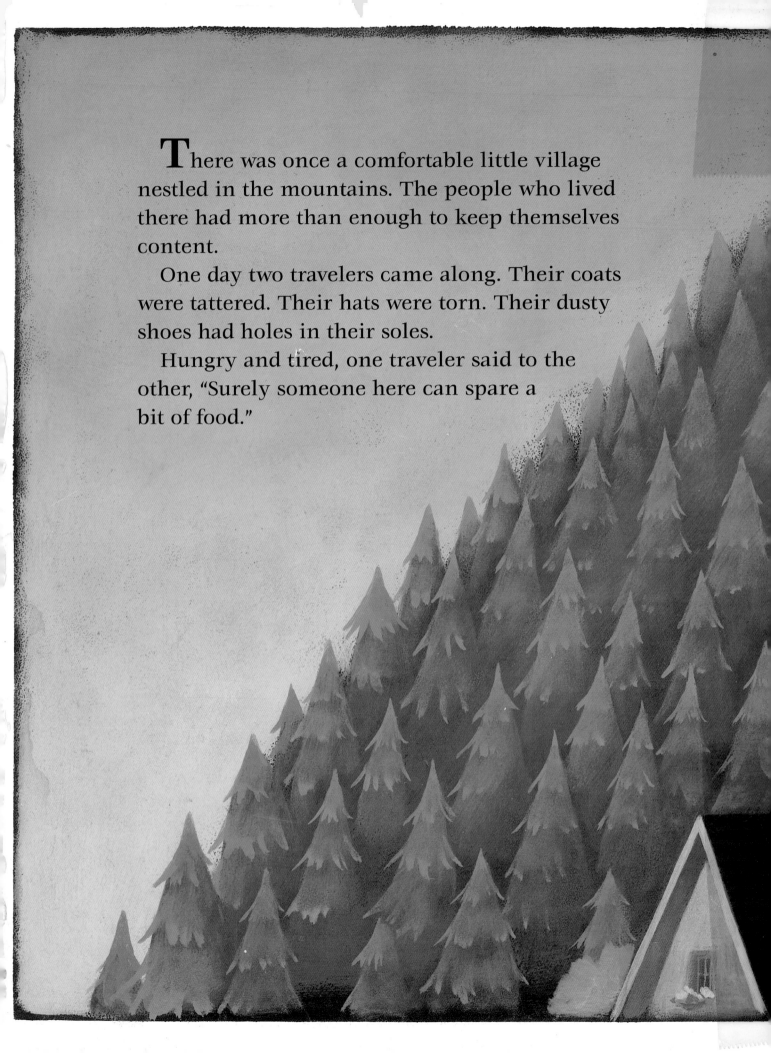

There was once a comfortable little village nestled in the mountains. The people who lived there had more than enough to keep themselves content.

One day two travelers came along. Their coats were tattered. Their hats were torn. Their dusty shoes had holes in their soles.

Hungry and tired, one traveler said to the other, "Surely someone here can spare a bit of food."

They knocked boldly on a door. It creaked open and a woman asked, "What do you want?"

"Please," said one of the travelers, "we are hungry. Do you care? Will you share? Do you have any food?"

The woman squinted her eyes and tartly replied, "No!" She quickly slammed the door shut.

The travelers walked a little farther down the road and knocked on another door. A young boy answered. His chocolate brown eyes were sweet. "Good day," he said shyly. "What do you want?"

"Please," said one of the travelers, "we are hungry. Do you care? Will you share? Do you have any food?"

The boy replied, "There is no food here" and closed the door.

The travelers wandered wearily through the village, knocking on every door. But everywhere they heard, "I don't care. I won't share. There is no food!"

They sat to rest beside a well. One traveler sighed and clutched his empty belly. He said, "If there is really no food in this elegant little village, then the people who live here are in greater need than we are. We should make them our magical soup."

The two travelers climbed up on the edge of the well and shouted, "We are master cooks! If anyone in this town has a big black pot, we will make the most delicious soup anyone ever tasted!"

A door slowly opened. A round man emerged carrying a gigantic black pot. "I love to eat!" he said. "Here's a pot. Let me see what two master cooks can do with it."

"Watch and see!" said one traveler with glee.

The travelers filled the pot with cold water and built a fire. Soon the flames licked the sides of the pot and billows of steam rose into the air. Curious people began to gather. "What is happening?" the townspeople asked.

"We are making an unusual soup," said one of the travelers. "It requires a special magical ingredient. I am certain we will find it in this town."

All the eyes in the crowd watched as one of the travelers reached down and picked up an ordinary stone. He tossed it into the pot with a splash. "We're making Stone Soup!" he said.

"It will be nutritious, delicious, incredible, and edible! But it would taste better," he paused and sighed, "if we only had a carrot."

"Where would we find a carrot in this town?" the other traveler asked. "We knocked on every door and everywhere we heard, 'I don't care. I won't share. There is no food!'"

"Then perhaps we cannot make the delicious soup after all," they both announced with a sad shrug of their shoulders, and began to turn away.

A child timidly raised her hand and said, "Wait! I might have a small carrot."

"Excellent!" shouted the travelers. "Bring what you've got! Put it in the pot! We're making Stone Soup!"

"This magical soup would taste even better if we had a potato," they added.

A deep voice in the back of the crowd called out, "I have a potato."

"Wonderful!" shouted the travelers. "Bring what you've got! Put it in the pot! We're making Stone Soup!"

"It would taste better still," they said, "if we had just a few more ingredients."

"Perhaps," said one villager, "I could bring a green bean."

"Well," said another, "if you are going to bring a green bean, I will bring a kernel of corn."

"I shall not be outdone," cried another. "I will bring an egg noodle!"

One by one, voices announced, "I will bring a slice of celery!" "I will bring a pinch of pepper." "I can bring a sprig of parsley!" "I might have a tiny turnip!"

"Well, why are you waiting?" cried the travelers. "Bring what you've got. Put it in the pot. We're making Stone Soup!"

Everyone in the town ran home to bring one small thing to put in the pot. Food flew through the air and landed with splashes in the growing soup. Soon the huge pot was full and simmering. A wonderful smell drifted through the air.

The smell was so tempting, people brought out bowls, spoons, chairs, and tables. They placed hearty loaves of bread, chunks of cheese, and bowls of fruit on the tablecloths.

Everyone came to taste the soup and marveled at the flavor. "It's amazing!" said one woman.

"These two travelers made such a delicious soup out of a stone."

"Out of a stone," said the travelers with a grin, "and a magical ingredient . . . *sharing.*"

As the travelers left the town they
said, "If anyone ever wants to make this
soup again, just remember the recipe.

Bring what you've got.
Put it in the pot.
Every bit counts,
from the largest to the least.
Together we can celebrate
a Stone Soup feast!"

How to Make Your Own Stone Soup

one large stockpot
a group of friends
one stone the size of an egg
two quarts of water
one quart of tomato juice
several carrots
an onion
a couple of potatoes
a couple of stalks of celery
a cup of peas

a cup of corn kernels
a tomato
a bunch of green beans
small pieces of broccoli
small pieces of cauliflower
a quarter-cup of uncooked pasta
a tablespoon of salt
a quarter-teaspoon of pepper
a loaf of bread
sharing

Set a time and place when friends can gather to cook together. Each friend brings some vegetables to contribute to the soup. Have several adults on hand to help with the cutting and pouring.

Pour the water and tomato juice into a large stockpot (liquid should fill it halfway). Wash the stone thoroughly and add it to the soup. Simmer the mixture on the stove until the soup bubbles.

Meanwhile, wash the vegetables and peel the carrots, onion, and potatoes. On a cutting board, carefully cut the vegetables into bite-sized pieces. Add the carrots, onion, potatoes, and celery to the pot and bring the soup back to a boil. Lower heat and simmer for 25 minutes or until vegetables are tender when pierced with a fork.

Add all the other vegetables and cook for 15 minutes more, stirring occasionally. Add the pasta and cook for another 7 minutes or until noodles are done. Season the soup with salt and pepper.

This recipe serves 10-12 adult-sized portions or 36 4-ounce-cup samples. To serve more people, use a bigger pot and more of everything. For variety, use other vegetables of your choice, add some crushed garlic during the last 10 minutes of cooking, or flavor the soup with a few pinches of dried spices such as dill, thyme, or parsley.

While the soup is cooking, sing songs and tell stories. When the soup is done, break the bread so that everyone has a piece. Serve the soup and enjoy a feast!